The PUMPKIN princess

The Hattan Company Ltd.
Unit 9 Overfield
Thorpe Way
Banbury
OX16 4XR
United Kingdom

www.thehattancompany.com

ISBN: 978-1-9160897-5-4

Illustrations by Xanthe Simmans.
The moral rights of the illustrator and author have been asserted.
All rights reserved.

For information about custom editions, premium or corporate purchases, please contact The Hattan Company Ltd. at contact@adamhattan.com

The Hattan Company

The PUMPKIN princess

**WRITTEN BY
ADAM HATTAN**

**ILLUSTRATED BY
XANTHE SIMMANS**

Beyond the mountains, across the rivers and further than the eye can see, is a teeny tiny kingdom with a royal family of three.

A King,

a Queen

and their daughter
of fifteen,

...rule over fields and fields
of pumpkins, oh so pristine.

From orange to white, from big to small, any kind of pumpkin
you can imagine, it's here you'll find them all.

But once a year
comes a very special day,
where the King and the Queen visit
the town, with something special to say.

One by one they knock on the doors along
the streets, each door with a pumpkin
outside inviting them in for treats.

The royal subjects know that on this, the festival
day, having a pumpkin outside the door,
is their way of saying 'hey!'

RAT-A-
TAT-
TAT

They knock on the doors with a rat-a-tat-tat.
And are invited in for pumpkin pie, hot chocolate and a friendly chat.

RAT-A-
TAT-
TAT

This year however, the Princess has turned sixteen. Now it's her turn to visit the town alone, and she's oh so keen!

She bids her parents goodbye and is off in a flash, down to the festival day with a skip and a dash.

She arrives at the first door and admires the pumpkin oh so round. 'This family knows a good pumpkin, what a pumpkin they've found!'

She brings up her hand to give a rat-a-tat-tat, but out of the corner of her eye, she thinks 'but wait, what's that?'

Just a few doors down, something catches her stare.
A green door without a pumpkin outside...
'Maybe they're not aware?'

'Maybe they've forgotten,
maybe they're shy,
maybe they're sleeping,
or maybe they ran out of pie?'

'Could they be new to the kingdom,
do they not know about today?
Maybe I'll go and say hello and
invite them out to play?'

Up to the green door she
goes and gives a rat-a-tat-tat.

'I hope they've got hot
chocolate, there's nothing
better than that.'

RAT-A-
TAT-
TAT!

A young girl answers with a face of pure disgust.

'WHAT DO YOU WANT?'

The young girl shouts.

'I DON'T LIKE TO BE FUSSED!'

'But it's the festival,' the Princess replies.

'I thought you might like to play? There's pumpkins aplenty and it's such a lovely day.'

GO AWAY!

'WELL I HATE PUMPKINS!'

The young girls says. 'HATE THEM I DO!

'TOO ORANGE,

TOO ROUND

...AND THEY SMELL
LIKE POO TOO!'

'Now I'm upset,' the Princess cries.

'I love pumpkins with all my heart.
They're the best thing about our kingdom,
the very best part.'

'WELL I HATE THEM!
I HATE THEM!
HATE THEM I DO!
AND YOU KNOW WHAT ELSE...

I HATE YOU TOO.'

The girl slams the door and the Princess falls back. She lands in a puddle of mud, her dress now covered in black.

The Princess bursts into tears and takes off in a hurry. Her day has been ruined and she wants to go home to Mummy.

But there's one thing the Princess forgot to do.
She didn't say hello to the subjects,
not a dozen, not a handful, not even a few.

The next year the Princess is ready to go back into to town.
She gives her parents a kiss and puts on her favourite gown.

Skipping down the hill, she's so excited to say hello.
'Nothing's going to ruin this year,' she thinks.
'Nothing like a year ago.'

GO PRINCESS!

But before the Princess
can give a rat-a-tat-tat, there's
something bothering her.
Whatever is that?

The green door with no pumpkin is what the Princess spies. No cheer, no smiles or invitation of pies.

DON'T STOP HERE!

RAT-A-TAT-TAT!

NO PUMPKINS!

STRICTLY NO VISITORS!!

But the Princess doesn't think as she walks up to the door, she gives a rat-a-tat-tat hoping the girl is nicer than before.

Again, the door slams and the Princess falls down.

Back to the castle she runs with tears and a frown.

Another year passes before the Princess is ready to try once more.

'She's got to be nicer this time,' she thinks.
'She's got to be nicer than before.'

Down the hill she goes, getting closer and closer to town.

'Something seems to be missing,' she thinks.

'Have the decorations been taken down?'

Get Your Pumpkins Here

But then, the Princess sees
no pumpkins outside the doors.
No music, no flags, none of what
she adores.

The Princess falls to her knees
as she begins to cry alone.

'Does no one like me now?
Is there something I should
have known?'

But then, the Princess spots a pumpkin sitting outside a home. It's a teeny tiny house, with a roof the shape of a dome.

The Princess dries her tears and walks up to the little house.

She gives a soft rat-a-tat-tat, almost like she's a mouse.

RAT-A-
TAT-TAT!

A friendly lady opens the door and invites her in for tea. 'Come in my dear, please. Whatever is the matter, what's the matter sweet pea?' The Princess tells her story of the girl behind the green door, how no one seems to like her now... She can't bare to say anymore.

'You see my dear' the lady starts. 'It's not that no one likes you, it's that you've broken their hearts. In focussing on the one person that doesn't like you, you've missed out on the people that truly do.'

'But what should I do?' The Princess asks. 'How can I repair their broken hearts?'

'You've just got to remind them that you really do care. Remind them that you never forgot, that they were always there.'

'Show them you're the Princess of their fine kingdom. Don't let someone's horrible words, affect your grace, your kindness, your wisdom.'

And so the Princess ran to the first door she could!
She hoped the family would answer, but who knows if they would.

RAT-A-
TAT-
TAT!

She gave a rat-a-tat-tat and
waited to see if they'd open up.

Luckily they did and they couldn't believe their luck.
'You came!' The daughter shouted with glee.
'We thought you'd forgotten about us,
we wondered where you could be.'

'I'm so sorry.' The Princess
said to the family. 'Don't be
silly,' the mother replied.

'You're here now
is what matters,
now please, do
come inside.'

Before long, the whole town was overjoyed to see their Princess return and the festival enjoyed.

Princess WE ♥ you!

The Princess danced and played with the people,

pumpkin Pals £6

little rascal

realising that someone's words, shouldn't stop you from being gleeful.

The friendly lady smiled as she saw the Princess play.
'Remember to treasure those who love you, no matter what others may say.'

'And now Pumpkin Princess, I leave you happy and well.
Ignore those that try to hurt you. Goodbye and farewell.'